Created by

Dedicated to
Max

Jake and his dummy

Jake feared those words that his mummy often said,
"You're a big boy now, you don't need your dummy for bed."

"But why can't I keep it? It helps me sleep."
"Instead try closing your eyes and counting sheep."

"Counting sheep? I'll never nod off,
my dummy stops me from having a cough!"

"Jake, no one has a dummy when they start school,
You don't want to be laughed at and look uncool."

"But it's my yummy gummy dummy that I suck and chew. It makes me feel safe and it's definitely not for you."

Mummy gave Jake his dummy and her face began to beam.
As her little man's eyes were getting heavy and he began to dream.

All of a sudden a frosty wind began to blow.
Jake had never seen so much snow.

He suddenly slipped and began to roll,
As he fell into a sign saying welcome to the North Pole.

Up he looked to see a big black boot
A long white beard and big red suit.

"It's Santa he whispered," giving the red jacket a tug,
Santa picked him up giving him a huge hug.

He took Jake inside and poured himself some tea.
He stretched out his hand and said, "Have you got something for me?"

"What do you mean?" Jake looked at Santa funny.
"Have you not come all this way to give me your dummy?"

"But it's my yummy gummy dummy that I suck and chew.
It makes me feel safe and it's definitely not for you!"

"Everyone gives their dummy to Santa when they grow up.
On Christmas Eve you leave it at your bedside in a little cup."

"But when you take it where does it go?"
"Well I bring it back here to my Christmas grotto."

All of a sudden Santa made appear
Thousands and thousands of baby reindeer.

"These babies take your dummy, but reindeer don't cry.
It gives them comfort but also helps them fly."

"Then once the reindeer suck it they feel content,
but at the same time they also pick up your scent."

"So when they grow up and take to the sky,
They'll be able to smell you and know which direction to fly."

Jake awoke and felt his dummy tucked up his sleeve, his mum came in and announced, "Jake! It's Christmas Eve".

She looked at Jake's face and said "oh darling what's up?"
"Nothing mummy but can you get me a cup?"

That night Jake left his dummy at the side of his bed, rolled over, closed his eyes and dreamt of Santa instead.

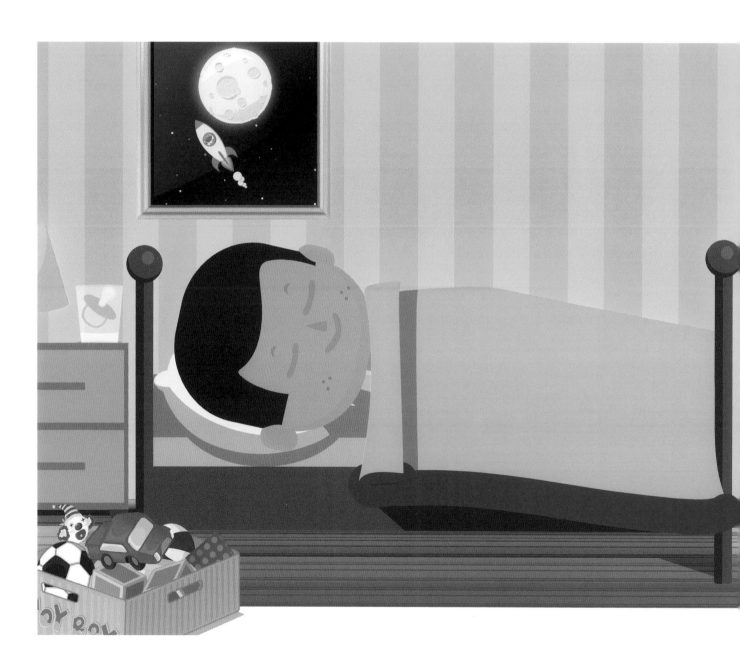

The End.

The End.

Story Quiz

How many dummies can you find?

How many reindeer can you find?

What does Jake call his dummy?

What was your favourite part of the story?

Answers: 22 Dummies. 14 Reindeer. His yummy gummy dummy.

Other titles by Baboon Books available now

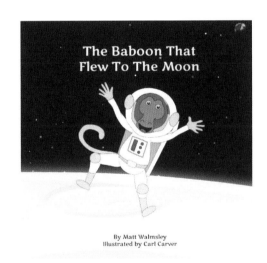

The Baboon That Flew To The Moon

Printed in Great Britain
by Amazon